Teachers, librarians, and kids from across Canada are talking about the *Canadian Flyer Adventures*. Here's what some of them had to say:

Great Canadian historical content, excellent illustrations, and superb closing historical facts (I love the kids' commentary!). ~ *SARA S., TEACHER, ONTARIO*

As a teacher–librarian I welcome this series with open arms. It fills the gap for Canadian historical adventures at an early reading level! There's fast action, interesting, believable characters, and great historical information. ~ *MARGARET L., TEACHER–LIBRARIAN, BRITISH COLUMBIA*

The *Canadian Flyer Adventures* will transport young readers to different eras of our past with their appealing topics. Thank goodness there are more artifacts in that old dresser ... they are sure to lead to even more escapades. ~ *SALLY B., TEACHER–LIBRARIAN, MANITOBA*

When I shared the book with a grade 1–2 teacher at my school, she enjoyed the book, noting that her students would find it appealing because of the action-adventure and short chapters. ~ *HEATHER J., TEACHER AND LIBRARIAN, NOVA SCOTIA*

Newly independent readers will fly through each *Canadian Flyer Adventure*, and be asking for the next installment! Children will enjoy the fast-paced narrative, the personalities of the main characters, and the drama of the dangerous situations the children find themselves in. ~ *PAM L., LIBRARIAN, ONTARIO*

I love the fact that these are Canadian adventures—kids should know how exciting Canadian history is. Emily and Matt are regular kids, full of curiosity, and I can see readers relating to them. ~ *JEAN K., TEACHER, ONTARIO*

What kids told us:

I would like to have the chance to ride on a magical sled and have adventures. ~ *EMMANUEL*

I would like to tell the author that her book is amazing, incredible, awesome, and a million times better than any book I've read. ~ *MARIA*

I would recommend the *Canadian Flyer Adventures* series to other kids so they could learn about Canada too. The book is just the right length and hard to put down. ~ *PAUL*

The books I usually read are the full-of-fact encyclopedias. This book is full of interesting ideas that simply grab me. ~ *ELEANOR*

At the end of the book Matt and Emily say they are going on another adventure. I'm very interested in where they are going next! ~ *ALEX*

I like when Emily and Matt fly into the sky on a sled towards a new adventure. I can't wait for the next book! ~ *JI SANG*

Flying High!

Frieda Wishinsky

Illustrated by Dean Griffiths

MAPLE
TREE
PRESS

Maple Tree Press Inc.
51 Front Street East, Suite 200, Toronto, Ontario M5E 1B3
www.mapletreepress.com

Text © 2007 Frieda Wishinsky   Illustrations © 2007 Dean Griffiths

Distributed in Canada by Raincoast Books
9050 Shaughnessy Street, Vancouver, British Columbia V6P 6E5

Distributed in the United States by Publishers Group West
1700 Fourth Street, Berkeley, California 94710

Dedication
To Helen and Reg Alev: Flying high over Chicago was awesome!

Acknowledgements
Many thanks to the hard-working Maple Tree team—Sheba Meland, Anne Shone, Grenfell
Featherstone, Deborah Bjorgan, Cali Hoffman, Dawn Todd, and Erin Walker—for their insightful
comments and steadfast support. Special thanks to Dean Griffiths and Claudia Dávila for their
engaging and energetic illustrations and design.

Cataloguing in Publication Data
Wishinsky, Frieda
Flying high! / Frieda Wishinsky ; illustrated by Dean Griffiths.

(Canadian flyer adventures ; 5)
ISBN-13: 978-1-897066-98-0 (bound) / ISBN-10: 1-897066-98-8 (bound)
ISBN-13: 978-1-897066-99-7 (pbk.) / ISBN-10: 1-897066-99-6 (pbk.)

1. Bell, Alexander Graham, 1847–1922—Juvenile fiction.
I. Griffiths, Dean, 1967– II. Title. III. Series: Wishinsky, Frieda. Canadian flyer adventures ; 5.

PS8595.I834F59 2007   jC813'.54   C2007-901862-9

Design & art direction: Claudia Dávila
Illustrations: Dean Griffiths

We acknowledge the financial support of the Canada Council   ONTARIO ARTS COUNCIL
for the Arts, the Ontario Arts Council, the Government   CONSEIL DES ARTS DE L'ONTARIO
of Canada through the Book Publishing Industry Development Program (BPIDP), and the
Government of Ontario through the Ontario Media Development Corporation's Book Initiative
for our publishing activities.

Printed in Canada
Ancient Forest Friendly: Printed on 100% Post-Consumer Recycled Paper

A   B   C   D   E   F

CONTENTS

HOW IT ALL BEGAN

Emily and Matt couldn't believe their luck. They discovered an old dresser full of strange objects in the tower of Emily's house. They also found a note from Emily's Great-Aunt Miranda: "The sled is yours. Fly it to wonderful adventures."

They found a sled right behind the dresser! When they sat on it, shimmery gold words appeared:

Rub the leaf
Three times fast.
Soon you'll fly
To the past.

The sled rose over Emily's house. It flew over their town of Glenwood. It sailed out of a cloud and into the past. Their adventures on the flying sled had begun! Where will the sled take them next? Turn the page to find out.

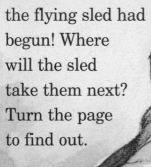

Silver Dart
Baddeck,
Nova Scotia
1909

1

First Up

Emily stared at the icicles above her window. It was too cold to play outside, but it was a perfect day for a sled adventure!

She ran downstairs to phone her friend Matt.

"I'll be right over," said Matt.

Emily peered out the living-room window as Matt skidded across the icy sidewalk toward her house.

"Yikes!" Matt shouted as he slipped and fell in front of her door.

Emily raced to the front door. "Are you okay?" she called.

"I'm okay. Just sore in my you-know-where." Matt hobbled to the door.

"Mom," called Emily. "Matt fell on the ice. Could you make some hot chocolate to help him feel better?"

Mrs. Bing poked her head out of the kitchen. "Two hot chocolates coming up."

Soon Matt and Emily sipped their drinks at the kitchen table.

"So, what are you two going to do today?" asked Emily's mother.

Emily and Matt looked at each other. What could they say?

"We'll probably fly on a magic sled," said Emily.

Matt's eyes widened. He couldn't believe what Emily was telling her mother.

Emily's mom laughed. "I love your imagination, Emily," she said.

"Thanks, Mom. And thanks for the hot chocolate. See you later."

"Be careful, you two," said Emily's mother, winking. "Don't fly *too* high."

"We won't," said Emily.

Emily and Matt raced up the creaky stairs to the tower.

Emily pushed open the tower door and hurried over to the dresser. She opened the second drawer and peeked inside.

"Look!" she said, pointing to a small wooden model airplane. It was labelled: *Silver Dart, Baddeck, Nova Scotia, 1909.*

"Wouldn't it be great to watch one of those old airplanes fly? I could draw a picture of it taking off," Emily said, pulling out the sketchbook she always carried in her pocket.

"And I could record what we see and hear," said Matt. He patted the pocket where he always kept his digital recorder. "Baddeck is beautiful. We went there last summer. It's where Alexander Graham Bell, the inventor of the telephone, lived. We visited a museum that was all about him. It would be awesome if we could meet him!"

"It would be awesome if we could use his telephone. I saw an old telephone in a museum once, too. It was big and black."

"So, what are we waiting for?" said Matt. "Let's go!"

2

More!

Emily and Matt hopped onto the *Canadian Flyer* sled. In no time, the magic words appeared.

Rub the leaf
Three times fast.
Soon you'll fly
To the past.

"Here goes," said Emily, rubbing the maple leaf on the front of the sled.

Soon they were enveloped in thick fog.

When the fog lifted, they flew over Emily's house, over their town of Glenwood, and into a fluffy white cloud.

When they burst out of the cloud, their clothes had changed. Emily wore a long red coat, a purple scarf, a hat, and high-buttoned brown boots. Matt wore a brown jacket, a blue cap, and brown boots.

Matt pointed to the ground below, covered with snow and ice. "I'm glad this jacket's warm. It looks as cold here as it was at home."

The sled bumped down on the snow. Emily and Matt slid off and peered around. They saw an old barn to their right, and people skating on a nearby lake.

"Let's hide the sled in the barn and find out where we are," said Emily.

Matt and Emily began to drag the sled. But before they could reach the barn, someone tapped Emily on the shoulder. Emily spun around.

A dark-haired girl of about five was staring at her. She wore skates and was dressed in a long navy blue coat and hat.

"Can I have a ride on your sled?" the little girl asked.

"It's very old," said Emily.

"I'll be careful," said the girl. "See?" And before they could stop her, the girl had plunked herself down on the sled.

"Ruby, get off that sled! It's not yours." An older boy with curly dark hair dashed toward them.

"Please, can I have a ride?" Ruby looked up at Emily and Matt with her big green eyes.

"Sure," said Emily. "But take your skates off first so you don't scratch the sled."

The older boy sighed. "You don't have to

give her a ride. She's a pest. She's always disappearing. I'm George McNeil, by the way."

"I'm Emily Bing, and this is Matt Martinez. We don't mind giving Ruby a ride."

George walked along as Emily pulled Ruby on the sled. "Are you visiting Baddeck to see the Silver Dart fly tomorrow?" he asked.

Emily nodded.

"My mother thinks that tomorrow, February 23, 1909, is going to be the most amazing day in Canadian history," said George. "But my father thinks it's going to be the biggest joke in the world. He thinks airplanes are silly contraptions."

"I love airplanes," said Emily.

"Me, too," said George. "Mr. Bell helped build the Dart, and he always has great ideas. Have you met him?"

Matt's eyes lit up. "No. Have you?"

"Once. I bet he's excited about the Dart flying tomorrow. The whole town is. Everyone will be here on the lake to see it. I'm taking pictures with my new Brownie camera. I can't wait to try it out."

"Come on," said Ruby, tugging at Emily's coat. "Stop talking so much. Go faster."

"Your turn, Matt." Emily handed Matt the sled's rope.

Matt pulled the sled.

"Faster!" cried Ruby.

"Hold on," said Matt, and he raced the sled across the ice.

Ruby giggled. "Faster! Faster!" she called, letting go of the side of the sled and clapping her hands. But as she did, the sled tipped over and spilled Ruby right onto the ice.

3

Ruby in the Way

George and Emily ran over to the sled. "Are you okay?" Emily asked.

Ruby and Matt were sprawled on the ice.

Ruby stood up first. "I'm fine," she announced. "Let's go again."

"I'm not fine," said Matt, rubbing his leg. "My leg got tangled in the rope, and my knee hurts. You were supposed to hold on, Ruby. The sled almost broke!"

"Sorry," said Ruby. "I'll hold on better now. This time, George can pull me."

George frowned. "No. I've had enough of chasing you all over this lake."

"You're mean," said Ruby, and she stomped off.

"I'd better follow her and make sure she doesn't get into any more trouble," said George. "But why don't you both come over to my house?"

George pointed to a three-storey red brick house not far from the barn and the lake. "It will be fun to be with friends my own age instead of Ruby."

"We'll come over soon," said Matt.

"Great!" said George. "See you."

Then he ran after Ruby.

"Hurry. Let's hide the sled in the barn," said Emily. "I don't want Ruby anywhere near it."

"I know. She almost broke it when I gave her a ride. If the sled breaks, we'll never get home," said Matt. He picked the sled up and carried it in his arms toward the barn.

"Do you think Ruby saw us heading for the barn before?" Emily pushed the old wooden barn door open. The barn was full of rusty farm equipment, bent shovels, and bales of hay.

"I don't think so. Anyway, who'd want to come in here? It's creepy, and it smells. I bet nobody's been inside this barn for years."

"Let's stick the sled under that pile of hay."

Matt carefully placed the sled under the hay and covered it with more hay.

Then Emily and Matt hurried outside toward the McNeils' house.

"Well, we know one thing for sure," said Emily. "The Silver Dart is going to take off from this lake, and we're going to watch it fly!"

"Maybe we'll even meet Alexander Graham Bell tomorrow," said Matt.

As they approached the McNeils' front steps, a woman in a tweed jacket stepped out. She had thick brown hair knotted in a bun and wore rimless glasses. She looked straight at them and smiled.

"Good day," she said. "Do I know you? I know everyone in Baddeck." The woman pronounced each word slowly and carefully.

"I'm Emily, and this is Matt. We're friends of George and Ruby."

"Then you must come for tea with them to Beinn Bhreagh this afternoon." She pronounced the name *Ben vree-ah*. "We're celebrating tomorrow's flight."

"What's Beinn Bhreagh?" asked Emily, saying the strange name carefully.

"The Bell family home," said the woman.

"Are you related to Alexander Graham Bell?" asked Matt.

The woman chuckled. "You could say that. I am Mabel Bell, his wife. I look forward to seeing you both later."

Mabel Bell waved and walked briskly down the road.

"Wow," said Matt. "I can't believe it. We just met Mrs. Bell! When we visited the museum in Baddeck, I read that she was deaf. But she understood everything we said. She's awesome at reading lips!"

4

Even Faster

Emily and Matt were about to knock on the McNeils' door, when it popped open.

"What took you so long?" said Ruby, grabbing Emily's hand. "Come see Flora, my new doll. She can open her eyes and blink."

"Ruby," said George. "They didn't come to see your doll. They came to meet Father and Mother, and play with me, too."

"Okay, but then they have to see Flora before we go over to Mr. and Mrs. Bell's house for tea."

"I was just about to tell you about that," said George.

"We met Mrs. Bell on our way in. She invited us to come to tea with you," said Emily.

"Terrific! Then you'll meet Bell's Boys."

"Are those his kids?" asked Matt.

"They're not his real kids. They're the four men who are part of the Aerial Experimental Association. They built the Silver Dart with Mr. Bell. Actually, there are only three men left. Thomas Selfridge was killed in a terrible airplane accident last year."

"Wow! Who's flying the Silver Dart?" asked Matt.

"Douglas McCurdy, and he's from right here in Baddeck," said George. "Come to the parlour and meet our parents."

The children trooped into the parlour, and George introduced Emily and Matt.

"We're delighted to meet you. George was telling us how patiently you gave Ruby a ride on your sled," said Mrs. McNeil.

"It was fun," said Ruby. "I want another ride later. Where's your sled?"

"We put it away for now," said Emily.

"Then give me a ride tomorrow," said Ruby. Emily and Matt glanced at each other. They were glad they'd hidden the sled.

"Ruby loves rides—on horses, on sleds, on anything. If it was up to our little Ruby, she'd be sitting beside young McCurdy tomorrow on that ridiculous airplane," said Mr. McNeil.

"I would if you'd let me," said Ruby. "I'd even take Flora. She'd love to fly, too." Ruby spun around the room. "We'd go up, up, up in the air!"

Mr. McNeil shook his finger. "I don't want you anywhere near that contraption, young lady. Airplanes have already killed one person, and even McCurdy had a close call last year. Airplanes are dangerous foolishness."

5

I Want to Fly

"Is that Beinn Bhreagh?" asked Emily as they climbed up a hill. She pointed to a large house full of turrets and towers.

"Yes," said Mrs. McNeil. "People say it's the most magnificent mansion in Eastern Canada. Wait until you see the views from inside."

"And wait until you meet Bell's Boys," said George. "I bet they're all excited about the flight tomorrow."

"I'm going to ask them if I can have a ride on their airplane," said Ruby.

"Enough of this talk, Ruby," said her mother. "I want you to promise to stay close to George while we're at the Bells'. I don't want you to hide in an upstairs wardrobe like you did last time. We were beside ourselves with worry until we found you."

Ruby giggled. "That was fun. I heard you coming, but you didn't know I was inside the wardrobe. It was full of dusty old coats, but I held my breath so I wouldn't sneeze."

Mrs. McNeil sighed as they walked up the front steps to the Bell mansion. "George, I'm counting on you to keep an eye on Ruby."

George groaned. "I'll try," he muttered.

"We'll all help keep an eye on Ruby," said Emily. "We won't let her out of our sight for a second."

Ruby stuck her tongue out at Emily.

"I saw that, Ruby," said her mother as

she knocked on the Bells' door. "Apologize to Emily."

"Sooo-rry, Em-i-ly," said Ruby. But Emily knew Ruby wasn't sorry at all.

A large man in a tweed suit with a thick white beard and a wide grin greeted them at the door. "Welcome," he said.

"Good afternoon, Mr. Bell," said Mrs. McNeil.

Emily and Matt stared at the large man. Alexander Graham Bell, the inventor of the telephone, was standing right in front of them!

"I'm delighted you're here," said Mr. Bell. "And how wonderful that you've brought these young people with you." Mr. Bell patted Matt and George on the back. He pinched Emily and Ruby on the cheek. "Tomorrow, children, you'll see something you'll remember for the rest of your lives. We're going to make history with the flight of the Silver Dart, right here from our beautiful Bras D'Or Lake!"

"Can I ride on the Silver Dart?" asked Ruby. She looked up and smiled sweetly at Mr. Bell.

Mrs. McNeil glared at her daughter. "Ruby!" she said sharply.

Alexander Bell guffawed. "I remember you, little lady. You visited a month ago. We had quite the time finding you. You like to hide in wardrobes, don't you? But I'm afraid there's room for only one person on the Silver Dart. Now, why don't you all come inside and have some refreshments?"

Everyone followed Mr. Bell into a large room.

From the windows Emily and Matt could see the frozen Bras D'Or Lake and the rolling hills and cottages of Baddeck.

About thirty people were in the room drinking tea, eating little cakes, talking, and laughing. It felt like a big birthday party.

Mr. Bell introduced them to a tall, dark-haired young man in his twenties. "This is Douglas McCurdy," said Mr. Bell, as proudly as if Douglas were his own son. "He will be flying the Silver Dart tomorrow."

Ruby tugged at Douglas McCurdy's sleeve. "I want to fly, too. Can I please have a ride on your airplane? I'll hold on tight."

"She's impossible," George said to Emily and Matt.

6

Santa Claus

"You know who Alexander Graham Bell reminds me of?" Emily whispered to Matt and George as they nibbled on little cakes.

"Who?"

"Santa Claus."

"You're right," said George. "He's big and round, and he has a beard. And he's very jolly."

"I wonder where he keeps his telephone?" asked Matt, looking around. "I don't see a telephone here."

"Me neither," said Emily.

"I didn't see a telephone around here the last time we visited," said George. "But maybe that's because we were all so busy trying to find Ruby."

Emily smiled. "Ruby is really a..."

"Nuisance," said George. "I'm glad you're both here. Maybe you could stay overnight with us. I asked Mother and Father, and they said it's fine. If you can stay over, we can walk to the lake together tomorrow to watch the Silver Dart fly."

"I think we can," said Matt.

"Let's go, children," said Mrs. McNeil. "It's been a lovely party, but it's time to head back."

"We'll check if we can stay over at your house," Emily told George and Ruby as they left Beinn Bhreagh. "We'll be back soon."

"Don't forget to bring your sled," sang Ruby. "I want another ride!"

Emily and Matt waved and raced toward the barn to check on the sled.

"I wish Ruby would forget about the sled," said Matt.

"I know. If she ever gets hold of it, she might ask someone else for a fast ride. And then our only way home might be smashed to bits."

"It's lucky the McNeils invited us to stay over," said Matt. "I was beginning to worry where we'd sleep tonight. That old barn would be ice cold at night."

"And stinky."

The sun was beginning to set as Emily and Matt hurried inside the barn. They ran to the bale of hay where they'd hidden the sled.

"It's here!" said Emily.

Matt pulled out his recorder. "This is Matt

Martinez reporting from Baddeck, Nova Scotia,
on February 22, 1909. Tomorrow we're going to
a frozen lake to see the first airplane in Canada
fly. Then—"

"Could you do that later, Matt? It's freezing

in here already. Let's hurry back to George and his family before it gets dark."

Matt snapped off his recorder and popped it into his pocket.

They ran all the way to the McNeils'. "I'm glad you can stay," said George, when he opened the door.

"Where's Ruby?" asked Emily.

"Mother sent her to her room early so she can rest up for tomorrow. She's even having dinner in her room. Isn't that great? We have time by ourselves without my pesky sister."

7

A Midnight Run

"What do you think?" George held up a small model of a wooden airplane.

"It's... It's...," stammered Matt.

It was the model airplane they'd seen in the dresser back home. But this one was missing one wing!

"I know it's not finished," said George. "I want to see the Dart tomorrow before I glue on the last pieces."

George's room was filled with models. Most of them were trains. They covered the top of his dresser, two shelves of his bookcase, and most of his desk.

"You're really good at making models," said Emily, admiring one of a caboose that sat on the bookcase.

"This one's hard though," George explained. "It's my first airplane model. I've seen pictures of the Dart but not the real thing. Tomorrow I'll see it for the first time!"

Mrs. McNeil knocked on the door. "Time for bed, children. Matt, you can sleep in George's room. Emily, you can have the guest room. It's the one next to Ruby's. Ruby is sound asleep already."

"Good night," Emily said to the boys as she followed Mrs. McNeil down the hall.

Mrs. McNeil handed Emily a long, flowery nightgown. "I know it's a bit long, dear. Be careful not to trip. Sleep tight."

Emily slipped on the nightgown and curled up under the cozy yellow and blue quilt. She pictured the Silver Dart taking off from the lake.

She yawned and closed her eyes. She could almost see the Dart flying higher and higher and....

What was that noise? Emily opened her eyes.

It sounded like someone fumbling with a doorknob. Someone was opening Ruby's door!

Emily sat up in bed. She glanced at the clock. It was midnight. Who was walking around at this hour?

Emily leaped out of bed and peeked out the door of her room.

Ruby was racing down the stairs in her coat and boots! She was heading for the outside door!

"Ruby!" called Emily. "What are you doing? Where are you going?"

But Ruby didn't answer. She zoomed out the front door.

Emily raced down the stairs after her. She grabbed her coat from the hall closet and slipped on her boots.

She stepped outside and peered into the darkness. She shivered. It was freezing outside. Maybe she should go inside and get help.

Emily turned toward the house but then she stopped. What if Ruby was going to the barn? What if Ruby had seen them hide the sled?

Emily didn't have time to get help. She had to find Ruby before anything happened!

8

A Promise

Emily raced across the cold ground. But just as she neared the barn, she tripped on her long nightgown.

"Ow!" she yelled. She'd banged her leg on the ice. Her leg stung but it wasn't bleeding.

Emily struggled to stand up.

"What are you doing here?" asked a small voice.

Emily looked up.

It was Ruby, dragging the sled by its rope.

"I was looking for you," said Emily.

"I went to get your sled. That way it will be ready for my ride tomorrow. Why did you hide it in that smelly barn anyway?"

"We wanted to keep it safe," said Emily.

"Because it can fly, right?"

Emily gulped. *How did Ruby know?*

"I saw you and Matt flying it the day George and I met you," said Ruby, as if she had just read Emily's mind.

"Ruby, does George know about the sled?"

"Nobody knows except me."

"You can't tell anyone. It's important."

"Okay. I won't tell. But can I fly on the sled?"

Emily took a deep breath. What could she tell Ruby? If she said no, Ruby might tell everyone about the sled.

But she couldn't let Ruby fly on it. What if it took her to the future?

"Ruby, I'm going to tell you the truth about the sled. It's magic, and Matt and I are from the future."

"Really and truly?" Ruby's eyes widened like saucers.

"Really and truly," said Emily. "Soon Matt and I will have to return to the future and we can't take you with us. So you can't fly the sled."

"But I want to. I want to so much."

"Look. I'll give you a long, fast ride on the ground tomorrow. I just can't let you fly the sled. Please understand."

"Promise to take me on a long, fast ride tomorrow?"

"I will. After the Dart goes up."

"Okay. I won't tell anything to anyone. But remember, you promised and you have to keep your promise."

Ruby pulled her coat tighter around her. "I'm cold. Now I want to go home."

"Me too," said Emily. "But let's put the sled back in the barn first."

They quickly returned the sled to the barn and then hurried back to the house.

"Goodnight, Emily," said Ruby. "Don't forget your promise."

"I won't."

Emily closed the door to her room and snuggled under the quilt.

Would Ruby keep her promise? What if she told everyone about the sled? What if she tried to make it fly?

9

Bell's Madness

The next thing Emily heard was someone banging on her door. She opened her eyes, slid out of bed, and went to the door.

Ruby stood there grinning. She was dressed in a long blue skirt and white blouse.

"Wake up, lazy bones," she said. "The Silver Dart is flying soon. And remember, you promised to give me a long ride on the sled after the Dart flies."

"When's it flying?" asked Emily, rubbing her eyes.

"This afternoon."

"But it's just morning now. There's lots of time."

"No, there isn't. The lake is full of people waiting for the Dart already. All the schools and stores are closed. The whole town is on the lake. We're all going to skate first. We've loaned Matt a pair of old skates, and we have a pair for you as well. Come on."

Emily dressed quickly and hurried to the dining room. After gulping down a bowl of porridge, she joined the others in the hall. George handed Emily a pair of skates.

"Let's go!" Ruby called, opening the front door. "Race you to the lake."

"I don't want to race," grumbled George.

"I do," said Ruby, and she tore out of the door, the leather straps of her skates dangling from her neck like a necklace.

"I'd better go after her," said George. He grabbed his skates and his Brownie camera.

Matt and Emily dashed after George toward the frozen lake.

The bright February sun sparkled on the ice.

"I wish I had sunglasses," said Emily, blinking.

"Look at the crowd!" exclaimed Matt.

The air buzzed with people skating, talking, and calling to each other.

"Here come Father and Mother," said George.

"I tell you, that ridiculous piece of metal and bamboo is not going to fly," said Mr. McNeil. "It's just Bell's madness. That man can't stop inventing new contraptions!"

"Now, dear. I'm sure Mr. McCurdy and Mr. Bell know what they're doing," said Mrs. McNeil.

"I'll believe it when I see it," said her husband, chuckling.

"Look!" cried Matt.

A horse and sleigh towed the Silver Dart onto the ice.

"There's Mr. McCurdy!" shouted Ruby. She began to skate toward him.

George skated after her and grabbed her arm. "Leave him alone," he said. "He has to

check the airplane. He doesn't want anyone annoying him."

"Stop squeezing my arm," wailed Ruby. "I'll leave him alone. I just want to see what he's doing to the airplane."

"Promise?" said George.

"Of course," said Ruby, flashing George a big smile.

10

Will It Fly?

George glanced at his watch. "It's almost three o'clock. When will the Dart fly?"

For the last hour the children had watched as Douglas McCurdy checked and rechecked every part of the airplane.

"What's he waiting for?" asked Matt.

A few minutes later they knew. A horse-drawn sleigh drove up, and out climbed Alexander Graham Bell dressed in a large furry coat. He marched over to McCurdy and put his arm around the young flyer.

"Are you ready?" Bell asked.

Douglas nodded and pulled his stocking cap tight over his ears. He stepped into the airplane, sat down, and signalled. Eight men hurried over to hold the airplane steady.

The crowd backed off as another man ran over and spun the propeller. The Dart's engine belched out a cloud of smoke and snow.

"I hope Mr. McCurdy knows what he's doing," said George. "It looks scary to go up in that airplane. He could fall out."

George, Matt, Emily, and Ruby stared as Douglas McCurdy gave another signal. The men holding the airplane let go and hurried out of the way. The Dart zoomed down the ice.

It moved faster and faster. But then, instead of lifting off the ground, it stopped. The crowd gasped. Douglas hopped out and scurried to the side of the airplane.

A few people in the crowd laughed. Mr. McNeil said, "I told you that contraption wouldn't fly."

But some people called out words of support. "Give the lad another chance!"

McCurdy ignored all the comments. He inspected the airplane carefully and fiddled with the gas pump. Then he asked the men to pull the airplane back to its starting position.

The crowd fell silent again. Everybody held their breath. Would the Dart fly this time or would it fail again?

The children's eyes were glued to the airplane as the propeller spun again. The engine revved up, and the Dart taxied down the ice. Faster and faster it sailed, but this time, like a giant bird, it rose in the air.

Cheers exploded from the crowd. Ruby jumped up and down. Matt and George tossed their caps and mittens into the air. Emily screamed, "Hurray!" and applauded until her hands hurt.

A bunch of boys skated after the airplane as Douglas McCurdy landed the Dart, a minute or so later, on the ice.

"Wow!" said Emily. "He did it! He really did it!"

"It was awesome!" said Matt.

"It was the most amazing thing I've ever seen," agreed George, snapping a picture with his camera. Then he turned around. "Ruby? Ruby? Where's Ruby?"

The children looked around but couldn't see her.

Matt pointed toward the airplane. "There she is!"

Ruby was talking to Douglas McCurdy and Alexander Bell. Douglas patted her on the head and lifted her up into the airplane.

"Look at me!" she called. She beamed as if she'd flown the airplane herself.

"She's impossible," said George. "She's just—"

"Ruby!" said Emily and Matt, chuckling.

"You're right," said George.

"I'm going to draw a picture of her on the Dart," said Emily. She pulled out her sketchbook and drew Ruby waving to the crowd like a queen.

11

Where Is She Now?

"Fly it again!" the crowd clambered for Douglas McCurdy to take the Dart up again.

"Well...," said Douglas.

Alexander Bell strode to his sleigh and stood up in it, facing the crowd. "Give the boy a rest," he said.

"I'll fly the Dart again tomorrow," Douglas promised.

The crowd applauded.

"Now," said Alexander Bell. "Everyone is invited to my laboratory for a reception to honour our brave young aviator, Douglas McCurdy."

"Look, George," said Ruby, showing him Emily's sketchbook as they climbed the hill. "Emily drew a picture of me on the Silver Dart!"

"Hey, that's good!" said George.

George held Ruby's hand as they followed the crowd into the laboratory.

It looked like the whole town was there. No one doubted that the Dart could fly now. But Mr. McNeil still did not like airplanes.

"McCurdy put on a good show," he said. "But what's the point of airplanes, anyway? Look how much trouble and money it took to fly one up for only a minute."

"One day airplanes will take you places fast," Emily told him. "One day you'll be able to fly to London, England, in only seven or eight hours on an airplane."

Matt nudged Emily. "Emily," he whispered.

Mr. McNeil laughed. "So you have a crystal ball to see into the future, do you, my dear?"

"No. I was just thinking that might happen," said Emily.

Mr. McNeil waved his hand as if dismissing Emily's remark. "Airplanes," he muttered. "Give me a good horse and sleigh over a piece of bamboo and metal any day."

Soon everyone hurried over to the long tables spread out with sandwiches and tea.

"I didn't realize how hungry I was, standing out there in the cold," said Matt, munching a chicken sandwich.

"Let's check on the sled soon," whispered

Emily. "Maybe it's ready to take us home. I don't want to sleep in that cold barn tonight."

Emily wanted to tell Matt that Ruby knew the sled could fly, but she couldn't tell him here or now.

"The sled will be fine," Matt reassured her. "I want to stay longer with George. Maybe we can stay one more night at his house."

Ruby ran over and tugged on Emily's sleeve. "When can I have my big sled ride?" Ruby asked.

Before Emily could answer, Matt said, "Never."

"Never? What do you mean never?" Ruby glared at Matt and Emily.

"What Matt means—," Emily began.

Matt interrupted. "You almost broke our sled, Ruby, and we don't want you on it again."

Ruby stuck her tongue out at them. "You'll be sorry," she said. And before Emily could stop her, she raced off.

12

Lost and Found

"Where's Ruby?" asked George, bounding over with his third sandwich.

"I don't know," said Matt. "She was here a minute ago and then she ran off when I told her she couldn't get a ride on the sled. She must be around here somewhere."

"Maybe she's outside," said Emily. "Let's check there." Emily was worried that Ruby might be so angry that she'd run all the way to the barn to get the sled. And then what would she do to the Canadian Flyer?

"Let's look inside first," insisted George.

The children hunted all over the Bell laboratory for Ruby. They called out her name. They looked in wardrobes and under tables, but they couldn't find her.

"We should look outside now," said Emily.

"Okay, but look at this!" said Matt. He pointed to a heavy black telephone on a table in a side hall.

Matt picked up the ear piece and talked into the mouth piece. "Hello? Hello?"

"Forget about the telephone," said George. "I have to find Ruby. I can't tell my parents that I've lost her again!"

"Follow me," said Emily. "I think I know where she is, and there's no time to waste!"

George ran to tell his parents that he'd meet them at home.

"Where do you think she went?" Matt asked.

"The barn," Emily answered.

"The barn? Why? You don't think she knows about the sled?"

"I know she does," said Emily. "Here comes George. I'll explain everything later. We have to hurry!"

George followed Emily and Matt out of the laboratory toward the barn.

But before they reached it, they saw Ruby. She was dragging the sled along the ice.

"Here's your flying sled," she said to Emily and Matt.

"What are you talking about, Ruby?" asked George.

"This sled can fly. It's magic."

George laughed. "That's a good joke."

"It really *is* magic. If I sit on it," said Ruby, plunking down on the sled, "I might make it fly!"

"Ruby, how about if I give you that long ride now?" said Emily.

"No. Flying will be more fun," said Ruby. "Come on, sled, up! Up!" Ruby patted the front of the sled like it was a dog.

Oh no! thought Emily. Ruby was rubbing the front of the sled so hard, she might make the words appear.

And then the sled would fly. Emily had to stop her!

Emily grabbed the sled's rope. "Come on, Ruby. We're going to fly along the ice."

Emily pulled the sled, racing along the ice as fast as she could.

Ruby giggled. "Hey, this is fun. It's almost like flying!"

Emily huffed and puffed. She was running so quickly she could barely catch her breath. Her legs were aching.

"We're stopping now, Ruby," she said after twenty minutes. "I kept my promise. I gave you a long ride and now you have to get off the sled."

"No," said Ruby. "Now I *really* want to fly."

"Ruby, we had a deal. Get off," said Emily.

Ruby shook her head. "No. I'm not getting off. I'm staying on this sled until it flies."

"Ruby, get off their sled," said George and he began to yank her off.

"Stop it!" Ruby screamed but George pulled her until she landed on the ice.

Ruby reached for the sled once more. Matt pulled it away, just as words began to form.

"Look, Emily!" cried Matt. He pointed to the words:

You watched the Dart
Soar toward the sky.
It's your turn now.
So say goodbye.

"Matt! Quick! Jump on!" Emily hopped on the sled. Matt jumped on behind her.

"We have to leave now. Remember us. We'll remember you," said Emily. She rubbed the maple leaf three times fast.

"B-but...," stammered George.

Ruby's mouth hung open, but she said nothing. For the first time since they'd met her, Ruby was speechless.

"Goodbye and thank you for everything!" called Matt, waving his cap as the sled rose above the lake, above Baddeck, and into a fluffy white cloud.

"Wow!" said Emily when they landed back in the tower.

"That was close," said Matt. "Do you think Ruby might have made the sled fly?"

"I don't know. It's lucky George pulled her off before anything happened," said Emily. "She really wanted to fly."

"I wonder if she ever flew on a real airplane."

"Maybe when she was much older. Not too many people flew in airplanes in those early days."

"Let's look at George's model again," said Matt. "Now that we've seen the Dart, I want to see if his model really looks like it."

Matt opened the dresser. Then he and Emily peered inside.

"It looks just like the Dart. George was great at making models," said Emily. "Look, Matt, there's a photograph beside the model. I don't remember seeing it there before."

"Me neither. It's a photo of a lady aviator near an old airplane."

"And there are words under the photo." Emily read the words aloud.

Ruby McNeil on her third solo flight in 1935.

"Ruby *did* fly airplanes! And all by herself!" exclaimed Emily.

"And look at the name of the airplane," said Matt.

Emily gasped as she stared at the words on the side of the small airplane:

The Flying Sled

MORE ABOUT...

After their adventure, Emily and Matt wanted to know more about Alexander Graham Bell and early flight. Turn the page for their favourite facts.

Emily's Top Ten Facts

1. Alexander Graham Bell's mother, Eliza Grace Symonds, was deaf.

2. Mabel Bell became deaf after getting scarlet fever when she was a child.

3. Mabel's mother encouraged her to learn how to read lips.

she was awesome at it! —M.

4. Alexander Bell met Mabel when he was teaching deaf children. They married on July 11, 1877.

5. Mabel Bell was smart and full of ideas. She organized the AEA (Aerial Experiment Association) to build airplanes, and even paid for it.

6. Mabel Bell wrote about her husband: "I never saw anybody who threw his whole body and mind and heart into all that interested him in a hundred different directions."

7. When Alexander Bell was upset about something, he often stayed up half the night playing the piano. When he played, his daughter Daisy said the big curl on top of his head wobbled.

8. Alexander Bell said "Hoy-Hoy" when he answered the telephone. He thought "Hello" was rude.

If I said "hoy-hoy" to my friends, they'd think I was nuts. —M.

9. In March 1909, French Baroness Raymonde de Laroche was the first woman to get an airplane pilot's license. In 1919 she tried to become the first woman test pilot, but her plane crashed and she and her copilot were killed.

10. In September 1910, Blanche Scott was the first North American woman to fly a plane alone. She was also the first woman to drive a car from coast to coast.

Matt's Top Ten Facts

1. Orville and Wilbur Wright made the world's first flight in a heavier—than—air machine on December 17, 1903, at Kitty Hawke, North Carolina.

2. Alexander Bell was interested in flight when he was working on the telephone. Tom Watson, who helped with the telephone invention, said that once Bell found a dead seagull. He measured its wings, guessed its weight, and checked out how its muscles worked. But he never noticed that it was dead and stank!

Dead seagull! P-U! -E.

3. Alexander Bell invented the telephone in 1876—he was only 29 years old.

4. Tom Watson said that if Bell had the money he would have used it to experiment with airplanes earlier. But all Bell's money went into fighting lawsuits about who invented the telephone.

5. Glen Curtiss, one of "Bell's Boys," once won the world speed record driving a motorcycle. He designed and built the motorcycle himself.

6. Thomas Selfridge was the first person killed in America while flying an airplane. He died on September 17, 1908, while flying with Orville Wright. Orville Wright was hurt but he didn't die.

7. Alexander Bell loved photographs and helped start the *National Geographic* magazine, which is famous for its photographs taken all over the world.

8. The Silver Dart—the first airplane to fly in Canada—was made of silver tubes, wires, friction tape, wood, and bamboo. It had no brakes.

No brakes!
Lucky it stopped!
-E.

9. The Brownie camera was invented in 1900. It only cost one dollar!

10. Bell's house, Beinn Bhreagh, means beautiful mountain.

So You Want to Know...

FROM AUTHOR FRIEDA WISHINSKY

When I was writing this book, my friends wanted to know more about Alexander Graham Bell, Douglas McCurdy, and the Silver Dart. I told them that *Flying High!* was based on real historical facts and that Douglas McCurdy, the Bells, and "Bell's Boys" were real people. I did make up many of the other characters such as Ruby, George, and Mr. and Mrs. McNeil. I also answered these questions:

Did Alexander Bell invent anything else besides the telephone and airplanes?

He invented an electric probe, which was used to locate bullets, a vacuum jacket to help sick people breathe, giant kites, and hydrofoils (boats that could lift high above the water as they sped around). Bell loved inventing. He said this about inventors: "You may give him wealth or take away all that he has, and he will go on inventing. He can no more help inventing than he can help thinking or breathing."

How did Alexander Bell meet Douglas McCurdy?

Douglas McCurdy's father was Alexander Bell's personal secretary. Douglas had been close to the Bell family since he was a child.

Why did the Bells establish the AEA (Aerial Experiment Association)?

Douglas McCurdy and his friend Frederick Baldwin, engineering students at the University of Toronto, decided to spend the summer of 1906 in Baddeck, Nova Scotia. One day they sat around with Alexander Bell talking about airplanes and aviation. Mabel Bell noticed how excited they all were and suggested they establish the AEA to build airplanes.

Did Douglas McCurdy fly any airplanes before the Silver Dart?

He flew his first airplane, the White Wing, in New York State in 1908. But as he took the plane up, he didn't see his friend Thomas and his dog walking nearby. He almost killed them! He also wrecked the airplane on landing.

Did his flying skills improve before he flew the Dart?

His flying skills improved a lot with practice and experience. He flew in Hammondsport, New York, where they built airplanes at Glen Curtiss' engine factory. McCurdy even flew the Silver Dart in New York before flying it in Canada in February 1909.

What did Douglas McCurdy do after he flew the Silver Dart in 1909?

He tried to convince the Canadian military that airplanes would be useful to them. He flew the Dart for them but they weren't impressed—especially when on the fifth flight, the sun blinded Douglas and the Silver Dart flipped over. He broke his nose and the airplane was wrecked.

What did McCurdy do after that?

He began a career as a "barnstormer"—a stunt pilot. He went to air shows and astounded people with tricks in the air. Many early aviators became stunt pilots. When he stopped flying (because he was having trouble with his eyesight), he represented aircraft companies. In 1947 he was appointed the Lieutenant-Governor of Nova Scotia. He died in 1961 at the age of seventy-four.

Did anyone ever build a model of the Silver Dart?

Between 1956 and 1958, the Royal Canadian Air Force built a replica of the Silver Dart. It flew again over the Bras D'Or Lake in Baddeck on the fiftieth anniversary of the first flight. Unfortunately the winds were strong and gusty that day, and this Dart crashed, too. It's now repaired and on display at the Canada Aviation museum in Ottawa.

Send In Your Top Ten Facts

If you enjoyed this adventure as much as Matt and Emily did, maybe you'd like to collect your own facts about Bell and early flight, too.

To find out how to send in your favourite facts, visit **www.mapletreepress.com/canadianflyeradventures**. Maple Tree Press will choose the very best facts that are sent in to make *Canadian Flyer Adventures* Readers' Top Ten Lists.

Each reader who sends in a fact that is selected for a Top Ten List will receive a new book in the *Canadian Flyer Adventures* series! (If more than one person sends in the same fact and it is chosen, the first person to submit that fact will be the winner.)

We look forward to hearing from you!

Coming next in the
Canadian Flyer Adventures Series...

Canadian Flyer Adventures #6

Pioneer Kids

Turn the page for a sneak peek.

From *Pioneer Kids*

Emily slipped into her seat as the class marched in. Then she opened her reader.

"Yuck!" she said. A dead black spider was splattered across the page. "I know who did this!"

Emily raced over to Luke's desk. She tapped him on the shoulder. Luke glanced up.

"What do you want?" he snarled.

"I'm not afraid of spiders. And I'm not afraid of you," she said. Then she turned, but before she reached her seat, a pebble hit her back. Emily spun around and stuck her tongue out at Luke.

"We have to do something about Luke," she said as she flopped back into her seat.

"Class, open your history books, and we will

take turns reading aloud," announced Miss Bridges. "Matt, you will have to share with Stefan again. Luke, begin reading."

Luke cleared his throat. "A long time ago…," he began.

"What's that smell?" Stefan whispered to Matt.

"I don't smell anything," said Matt.

"Look out the window! There's smoke near the barn!" Stefan leaped out of his seat. "Fire!" he shouted. He raced outside toward the barn.

Emily and Matt ran out after him. They grabbed buckets from the shed, filled them with water from the well, and threw the water at the flames.

"More water!" cried Emily. "Hurry! Our sled's in the shed beside the barn. We can't let it burn!"

As Emily and Matt tossed water at the

flames, they heard students screaming inside the school. They heard Miss Bridges, too.

"Stay calm, class. Everyone, outside quickly." The students and Miss Bridges spilled out of the classroom.

"Grab buckets and sacks and help put out the fire," Miss Bridges said. "Quickly!"

Miss Bridges and some of the children filled buckets with water and tossed water on the flames. Others grabbed the burlap sacks piled at the back of the school. They dipped the sacks in water and slapped them against the flames.

The wind kicked up and blew the flames higher and closer to the barn. From inside, they could hear Luke's horse neighing.

"Prince is in the barn!" yelled Luke. "We have to save him. We can't let him die! Please. Please help him! I...I...didn't mean it. It was an accident!"

The *Canadian Flyer Adventures* Series

#1 Beware, Pirates!

#2 Danger, Dinosaurs!

#3 Crazy for Gold

#4 Yikes, Vikings!   #5 Flying High!

Upcoming Book

Look out for the next book that will take Emily and Matt on a new adventure:

#6 Pioneer Kids

And more to come!

About the Author

Frieda Wishinsky, a former teacher, is an award-winning picture- and chapter-book author, who has written many beloved and bestselling books for children. Frieda enjoys using humour and history in her work, while exploring new ways to tell a story. Her books have earned much critical praise, including a nomination for a Governor General's Award in 1999. In addition to the books in the *Canadian Flyer Adventures* series, Frieda has published *What's the Matter with Albert?*, *A Quest in Time*, and *Manya's Dream* with Maple Tree Press. Frieda lives in Toronto.

About the Illustrator

Gordon Dean Griffiths realized his love for drawing very early in life. At the age of 12, halfway through a comic book, Dean decided that he wanted to become a comic book artist and spent every spare minute of the next few years perfecting his art. In 1995 Dean illustrated his first children's book, *The Patchwork House*, written by Sally Fitz-Gibbon. Since then he has happily illustrated over a dozen other books for young people and is currently working on several more, including the *Canadian Flyer Adventures* series. Dean lives in Duncan, B.C.